John Alfred Langford

Heroes and Martyrs

And other Poems

John Alfred Langford

Heroes and Martyrs
And other Poems

ISBN/EAN: 9783744765190

Printed in Europe, USA, Canada, Australia, Japan

Cover: Foto ©Andreas Hilbeck / pixelio.de

More available books at **www.hansebooks.com**

HEROES AND MARTYRS.

HEROES AND MARTYRS

AND

OTHER POEMS

BY

JOHN ALFRED LANGFORD, LL.D.

𝕷𝖔𝖓𝖉𝖔𝖓

T. FISHER UNWIN

PATERNOSTER SQUARE

MDCCCXC

To

MY LIFELONG FRIEND,

JOHN S. MANTON,

THIS VOLUME

IS

AFFECTIONATELY DEDICATED.

CONTENTS.

viii

HEROES AND MARTYRS

AND OTHER POEMS.

—✦—

JOHN ROGERS.

Burned, *February* 4, 1555.

———

The end is near. O Lord, my God, be praised,
The end is near ; the end for which I prayed :
And now the martyr's crown will soon be mine.
But one more blissful night and then will break
The still more blissful morn, whose welcome light
Will be the dawn of everlasting life.
Then from this narrow cell, these prison walls,
As well as from the prison walls of flesh,
My soul, made clear and purified by fire,
Will rise into the mansions Christ prepared,
The sinless habitations of the blest.

O God, sustain me : give me strength to bear
Whatever pain the burning may inflict.
Let not the shrinking flesh and feeble tongue

B

Incite the mockery of the jibing foe,
And make them rail on Thy most holy cause,
Moved by the weakness which I else might show.
But let Thy glory shine upon my face,
As in his death it erst on Stephen shone,
To fix the wavering, to confirm the strong,
And draw the wanderers from their erring ways
To Thy true fold ; unto Thy Christ and Thee.
So let Thy hand support me at the stake,
And as the fierce devouring flames arise
And fold me round, oh, let them to me cling
But as the marriage garments to a bride,
Where pain at parting from her earliest friends
Is lost in pleasure that she's found her lord.
In that dread moment when the torture most
Shall rend the sinews, and shrink up the flesh—
When life and death are in their final throes—
O Lord, let then my mind be full of Him,
Thy blessed Son, who died upon the cross,
That we might conquer sin and death, and live :
And this sustaining thought will give me strength,
Like Him, to bear; and, oh, like Him, forgive.
    All day, here sitting lonely in my cell,
I've seemed to live my life again. Once more
The past, from childhood to the present hour,
Rose visibly and clearly to my mind;

And from the secret chambers of the brain,
The angel memory recalled the days
Which have been, and the things which they
    brought forth.
And this my cell was peopled with a throng
Of noble-hearted men—the guides of youth,
The friends of manhood, and the hopes of age ;
Some who have fought already the good fight ;
And some who soon will follow in my track.
I trust to die so that my death may prove
A light to light them on their perilous way.
    And then, methought, I was a boy again
In that bright Midland town where I was born.
Again I on the little foot-bridge stood
Where I so oft had been, and watched the stream,
That truest type of life.   Again I heard
The ever-rippling Rea's pellucid waves
Make sweeter music on the shining stones,
As still they brightly flow across the street,
The sunbeams dancing on them as they flow.
And here and there the restless minnows dart
In shadow-making shoals, as swift as thought
Succeeds to thought within an active brain.
Again, upon my feet, I feel with joy
The cool refreshing waters as therein
I paddle up and down in summer-time,

Between the gardens, which, on either side,
Make beautiful the banks with plants and flowers,
The favoured haunts of butterflies and bees.
Or in the meadows and the fields I roam,
Or, dreamfully reposing on the grass,
The daisy-chains and cowslip-ball prepare,
To carry home, with childhood's pure delight,
The beauty and the fragrance of the fields.
Or in the park, beneath the stately trees,
At eve I lie, and watched the dappled deer
Majestically marching to and fro,
The many-antlered monarch at their head—
A sight to make the old man young again,
As ev'n its airy vision makes me now.
Once more with boy-friends hold I solemn talk
Of things which in our manhood we shall do :
But with the boys I only rarely played,
I was too fond of learning, and the school.

　My schoolboy days ! 　O days of sanguine hopes
When all the future seemed a golden path
Which led unto the promised goal. 　My heart
Was all athirst for knowledge, and I drank
From every spring from whence its waters flowed.
But mostly for the knowledge of God's Word,
The sacred strains of prophets and of saints,
My inmost nature yearned. 　Then days and nights

I o'er the holy volume pored, and heard
Sweet angel-voices calling me to God ;
Revealing the dark errors of the Pope,
The evil teachings of that Anti-Christ,
Which bound the mind in superstitious chains
And 'twixt the soul and her Redeemer placed
A man corrupt, and a debasing church,
Which still held all the Gospel would have freed
In bondage unto false and grovelling rites,
And doctrines leading but to death and hell.

For this great work it was my happiness to live
In a most blesséd time, and blesséd place :
For into Birmingham, by God's dear love,
The glowing light from Lutterworth had streamed,
And Wyclif's living words had fired the hearts
Of men and women who together met
To read the Word, which he, for this inspired,
Had turned into the common English tongue,
That all might read and know the will of God—
Most precious blessing yet bestowed on man.

The good seed grew ; and in a little time
These pious souls combined, and raised the means,
And built a house to God : a holy house ;
One free alike from Bishop and from Pope.
To which themselves their Pastor should select,
And after their own hearts the Preacher choose.

In this dear place the Gospel truth was taught,
The doctrine Christ to His Apostles gave,
Unmixed with superstition, and the snares
Which dark traditions round the simple words
Had woven to delude, mislead, deceive, betray :—
Again the ransomed spirit to enthral,
And quench the lamp the Saviour had illumed.
From this reopened spring of purest grace
I drank unslakingly : my faith grew strong.
Thus day by day I still more clearly saw
That Rome was Anti-Christ : that all her power
Was based on ignorance, idolatry, and fraud ;
Her promises delusions ; and her boast
That in her hands she held·the keys of heaven ;
Could pardon or condemn ; could bind or loose ;
And was the one sole source of heavenly grace,
Was vain and empty as a maniac's dream.
For me, henceforth, one source of truth remained,
One only source—the precious Word of God.
This Word I got by heart ; its language learned,
And prayed to gain its spirit, so that I,
Whatever persecution should devise,
Might never falter in my upward way ;
But like a soldier of the Cross endure
Even to the end : and now that end is here,
Or will be with the dawning of the morn.

Then came those dear laborious years when I
At Cambridge wore the cap and gown ; and there
Obtained that learning which my nature craved,
And gaining which all labour was delight.
There every hour in study I employed,
And day by day still adding to my store
Full soon I mastered all my teachers knew,
Who praised my zeal, and my success proclaimed.
Then in the silent watches of the night,
Alone with my own heart and God, I still
The study of the Holy Book pursued,
And lived an inner life of faith and prayer ;
For ever hearing my great Master's voice,
And ever ready to obey His call.
That call came soon ; in sooth, almost as soon
As I was made a priest.   For at that time
Our merchants, who at Antwerp held their mart,
Made me the Chaplain of their English church'—
For which they have my prayers.
                                 ' O blesséd time !
Without presumption ; in true humbleness ;
In heartfelt gratitude, and prayerful praise,
I recognize God's guiding hand in this.
He led me to this hospitable place,
And to the men who made it sacred ground—
Our two bright, never-failing Gospel stars,

Good William Tyndal and Miles Coverdale.
He called me in their holy work to help,
To trim again the lamp by Wyclif lit,
That all the coming generations may
Behold the light, and follow where it leads.
The light enshrined in God's most holy Word,
By papist power was hidden in a tongue
Not by the people understood; but now
These noble two have made it plain and clear;
Revealed it to the world ; have turned it all
Into the English tongue, the common speech
Of all the people in our land.   And I—
O God, to Thee I render thanks and praise,
That Thou hast deemed me worthy such a work,
Hast joined my hand with theirs, and blessed my
    life
With this most precious token of Thy love !
  And now the work is done.   The Word will
    spread.
Oh, spread it, Lord !   Let knowledge so increase,
That every man and woman and little child—
The ploughman, and the weaver, and the smith,
And all who labour for their daily bread,
May soon this blessèd message read, and learn
That everlasting life is Faith in Christ :
The life, the truth, the way.

Thus looking back,
It seems God showered His blessings on me here,
And ev'n to overflowing filled my cup.
For here I found a true and loving wife,
Whose heart e'er beat in sympathy with mine ;
Who cheered my labours, and increased my joys ;
Made sunshine in our home, and blessed our
    hearth
With children's prattle and their guileless ways,
Which ever knit more closely married hearts,
And win a special blessing from our Lord,
Who little children blessed with those sweet words,
" Of such is heaven's kingdom "—and to us
They angels seemed, made beautiful our house,
And sanctified it for ourselves and friends.
O loving wife, O darling tried and true,
Joy of my joy, and sharer of my woe,
My only sorrow now is leaving thee,
And those dear offsprings of our happy lives.
But thou would'st have me ever keep my faith,
Nor by the heart's affections weakly swayed
To bow before the idol we have spurned.
Thou with thy prayers wilt strengthen me to bear
The fiercest tortures, rather than betray
Through craven cowardice the cause of Christ.
For well we know to all that thus shall die,

Our Lord the mourning widow will protect,
Will to the fatherless a Father be.
St·ll, cruel is the power which now forbids
That I should see and bless them ere I die.
    Once more the Gospel light on England shone,
And made the happy island beautiful.
The holy boy king, the Sixth Edward, reigned.
The Church was purified ; the Bible loved ;
And now translated in the common tongue,
In every church the precious Book was placed,
That all might read, or have its message read.
Good Bishop Ridley called me home again,
To bear my portion in the glorious work,
And labour in the vineyard of the Lord.
Then honours came to me from royal hands,
But with the honours heavier duties came :
The deep responsibilities of lofty place.
But still in singleness of heart I strove,
As ever in the presence of my God,
To do His will ; the great reward to win
˙Which comes from raising men from earth to
        Christ.
Nor all unfruitful was my work.   I felt
The Lord was with me in my daily task.
And now, imprisoned in this murky cell,
I see the great white throne, and all the saints,

And angels, cherubin and seraphin
That crowd around it giving praise to God !
   Then, for our trial, evil days returned.
The saintly king, the young and pious king,
Was summoned to resign his earthly crown,
To wear a still more glorious crown in heaven.
Now Mary reigns ; the Gospel is withdrawn.
God's precious Book, and God's most holy men,
Are given to the fire.   The papal crew,
Again triumphant, harry all the land,
Its soil enriching with its purest blood.
Yet one remembrance makes my heart rejoice.
I first of all God's servants was allowed
To bear my testimony to His truth.
For called before her Majesty to preach,
This poor weak frame was strengthened to resist
The terrible temptation of the place,
And of the congregation gathered there.
But God upheld me in that trying hour.
I saw nor Queen, nor courtiers, only God.
I did not shrink nor falter there ; nor force
My tongue to utter truth-betraying words ;
But spoke right out the doctrine I believed.
Denounced the Pope, the images, the mass,
Idolatry, and superstitious rites ;
All vain and foolish trust in empty works ;

Declared salvation only could be found
By faith in Christ, and in His Holy Name,
As in the blesséd Gospel is revealed.
And may its light, I said, with us remain,
And spread till it embraces all the realm !
And so I bore my witness for the truth.

For this before the Council I was called
And soundly rated.   Still, I did not quail.
Once more, and with a strength that was not mine,
Before them all I pleaded with a power
That silenced my stern foes.   I was dismissed,
And for a little time remained in peace.
Again they summoned me, and charge on charge
Of heresy and schism, in bitter terms
Was urged against my teaching and my life.
Of all my sacred work I was deprived ;
Condemned to silence ; in my house to live
A prisoner till their purpose was made known.

But martyr-making Bonner haled me out ;.
He enemy alike of God and man.
From wife, from children, and the sweets of home,
He had me dragged, and into Newgate cast,
Condemned with murderers and thieves to dwell.
But ev'n in this God's providence is seen,
For unto many I have shown His love,
And some have rescued from a death in sin.

And, as to holy Peter in his gaol,
Have angels come and glorified this cell,
And made this gloomy habitation seem
To me an ante-room of Paradise.
　　To-morrow I must die.　But little time
Is left me now on earth : and meet it is
I seek renewal of my strength in sleep.
I would not by the slightest weakness show
A touch of fear ; nor without cheerfulness,
Nor that deep inward confidence I feel,
Receive the crowning glory of my life.
O Lord, be with me in the final hour
That all may see how well Thy servants die.

————

　　Beside his wretched bed he knelt and prayed.
Then as a labourer wearied and outworn,
Who must at dawn resume his daily toil,
The trusting soul passed into deepest sleep.
Then on the morrow, smiling and serene,
He sealed his martyrdom and gained his crown.

SIR WALTER RALEIGH.

BEHEADED, *October* 29, 1618.

My life's long pilgrimage draws near its close;
And all its strange experiences by sea and land;
Its wonderful adventures, gladly sought,
Both in the old world and the new, where'er
New knowledge, new possessions might be won,
Are now but memories of a golden past,
For on my stage the curtain soon will fall.
And now how vividly before me rise
The thoughts of all that I have seen and done.
Not ghost-like, or as things beheld in dreams,
Creations of a dull disordered brain,
But full of life, of beauty, and of strength,
And moving me as in the far-off days
I grappled with them in the strength of youth.
So I re-live my life.
     A boy once more
O'er Devon's fair and story-famous fields,
Or by the ever-fascinating sea,
My blood a-tingle with the fires of health,
I rambled uncontrolled: my hopes sustained
By splendid visions fancy conjured up
Of great deeds I would do when manhood came—

That time by boys so sanguinely desired.
From sailors and from fisher-folk I heard
The charms and perils of a life at sea,
And of the wondrous lands that lie beyond.
Their every word as eagerly I drank,
As weary travellers in a thirsty land
Drink from a suddenly discovered well.
To every tale my heart responsive beat.
Each act of heroism, manly fortitude ;
Of dangers bravely met and overcome ;
Of sacrifice of self for noble ends,
Made all my pulses throb ; and I resolved
To do and dare ; to conquer or to die.
    And then my student days ! My rapt discourse
With those selected ministers of God,
The world-embracing poets, whose deep songs
Have so entranced my heart, so fixed my love, .
That they have long become a part of me.
With these and with divine philosophy,
How swiftly flew the golden-wingéd hours,
With music and with wisdom richly fraught !
And oft, as love and nature prompted them,
My thoughts would syllable themselves in song,
And ease my heart as birds do in the spring.
Then o'er the varied story of mankind,
The records of our great humanity,

Of every race and clime, I pondered much.
Their governments, their customs, manners, laws,
With all that makes a nation's life.   But most,
With loving sympathy my heart reviewed
The annals of my own immortal land,
Most glorious in arms, in arts, and song,
The wonder and the admiration of the world.
For her achievements done in freedom's cause ;
The greatness and the glory of her state,
Not to be paralleled in any age
By all the mightiest empires of the past.
    From College to the Temple then I passed ;
From poesy to law.   But my young heart—
Although I failed not in my profit there—
For wider fields and more excitement yearned,
And for the sword the gown I soon exchanged,
Resolved to strike a blow for fatherland,
And in the field to meet my country's foes ;
To smite the cruel Dagondom of Spain.
Nor was the aspiration air.   The blow
She aimed at England amply we repaid,
With usury multiplied a hundredfold ;
Her proud Armada met and overcame,
And with the fragments sowed the sea.   O those
        days !
On sea and land ; in Flanders and in France ;

I tasted the extremes of life, and felt
The ecstasy of peril.   Even now
Return the horrors I beheld in Paris,
On St. Bartholomew's most bloody day,
When led and prompted by the King and Court,
And by religious bigotry inspired,
And maddened with a diabolic zeal,
The Catholics rose against the Huguenots.
Then red assassination stalked the streets,
Broke into homes, nor ev'n the temples spared,
Till streets, and homes, and temples had become
Like slaughter-houses reeking with the blood
Of brothers by their brothers shed.   O God !
To think that this unnatural tragedy
Was perpetrated in Thy holy name !
Was sanctified, commemorated, blessed,
By him who claims by right divine to be
The head of Thy most holy Church ! .
　　　　　　　　My thanks and praise
To Thee, O Lord, I render once again,
That I, ev'n as it were by miracle,
In that most awful massacre, was saved,
That hellish carnival of death !
　　　　　　　　　　But now
A brighter incident arrests my thoughts.
I see our great and glorious Queen again.

C

Magnificent, majestic, born to rule,
A queen from head to foot.   With brain to plan,
And heart to execute the bravest deeds.
A man in counsel ; woman in her moods ;
And dowered with a graciousness which won
The heart-felt loyalty, devoted trust,
And still increasing love of all who came
Beneath the spell of her rich influence,
Till life without her favour worthless seemed,
And those were honoured best who served her most.
Then came the day of days, that golden hour,
That moment still by memory preserved
Through all the moments, hours, and days since
        passed,
When first I won her gracious smile, and felt
Her royal gaze upon me kindly fixt,
As o'er the mire my jewelled cloak I spread
That all unsmirched her royal feet might pass.
A momentary impulse prompted me.
And instinct often is a better guide
Than reason slowly moving on its way,
And losing what it toils for.   Thus I won
The notice and the favour of the Queen.
    But, oh, most vividly of all return
The soul-absorbing hours, the matchless time
I with the gentle-hearted Spenser passed ;

That calm meandering river of sweet song.
The Muses' favourite, well-beloved child;
The chosen of Apollo to restore
The golden days of poesy again,
And from the English lyre draw richest strains
And show how full of sweetest melody
Is England's tongue, and fitly celebrate
Her virgin ruler in his " Faery Queen."
Of chivalry, of knighthood, and of love,
Of chastity, of temperance, justice, truth,
Of perilous adventures worthy men
Who sought to stablish honour's rule on earth,
Of noble deeds for noblest purpose done,
Of virtue still triumphant over vice—
Such glorious themes inspired his holy song
And made his poem the pattern and the pride
Of all heroic souls; his knights the types
Of all true Christian gentlemen, which he,
Their singer, was in very truth.   A man
Whose talk was sweeter than his song; a man
Of noblest aspirations, purest souled,
In mind and body harmoniously complete.
May it be mine, in those Elysian fields
To which my soul is bound, to meet with him,
To walk and talk with him; to hear once more
That silver tongue in sweetest accents flowing,

Hold high discourse upon philosophy,
Religion, justice, virtue, beauty, truth,
And song, supremest teacher of them all !
Who would not gladly pass thy portals, Death,
To know such pure felicity as this ?

But for adventures still my bosom yearned.
I hungered to behold that brave new land
Columbus found for us.   And soon my sails
The broad tumultuous Atlantic knew.
With sanguine hearts and souls prepared to brave
Whate'er of good or evil Fate might bring ;
The good receiving with due thanks and praise,
The ill without complaint, we onward bore
Through storm and calm alike by hope sustained,
And reached the western world, new countries
    found,
And that rich part on which I first set foot,
Virginia, from our Virgin Queen, I named.
Not much of gold, but treasures thence I brought
Surpassing in their worth Golconda's mines—
The floury root to be the food of man,
And that rare weed, which through all coming times
For comfort and for solace he shall use,
And with its use the name of Raleigh bless.

But dark and direful days to England came.
Our royal paragon had passed away.

The great Elizabeth had ceased to reign.
The woman-man the man-woman's sceptre held,
And Spain had domination in her court,
Whose deep and subtle hatred wrought my fall.
By secret machinations and by fraud—
The king a ready minister in this—
For all who hated freedom hated me—
An accusation false as hell was made ;
With contemplated treason I was charged ;
To trial brought, and yet no trial had,
No evidence produced disclosing guilt,
But by the foul-tongued Coke, with heart as
    foul,
With fierce invective was my life assailed
And most disgraceful names against me hurled,
To blacken and degrade, my judges move
By prejudice and passion ; but undisturbed
By this vile practice, calmly I heard all.
Too often death had my familiar been,
To fear him now ; and though I loved my life,
Would guard it but by honourable means.
And in this temper my defence was made.
But for the pre-condemned defence is vain ;
The whitest innocence will naught avail.
And I was guilty found ; condemned to death ;
Left to the merciless mercy of the king.

But so flagitious was the sentence deemed,
The people's sense of justice so outraged
By this display of Spanish hate and power,
They dared not carry the vile sentence out,
But left me in the Tower.   From year to year,
Through fourteen revolutions of the sun,
A prisoner condemned I lived my life.
But prison walls cannot confine the soul,
The soaring spirit kill.   I lived my life.
And drawing from the annals of the past,
And from the wealth of wisdom stored in books,
And from the gracious studies of my youth,
I made a palace of my prison home,
And peopled it with all the great and good,
Whose noble actions are the themes of praise.
And thus inspired I laboured on, and wrote
My prison book, " The History of the World "—
My legacy bequeathed to men unborn.
And oft I seemed to hear my Spenser's voice
Repeating as of old his honied strains ;
And saw his gentle face, his gracious smile,
Imparting hope, encouragement, and strength.
   But oft the spirit of my youth returned.
I longed once more to breast the rolling seas,
To breathe once more the fresh free air of heaven,
And new adventures seek.   To that new world,

Which is a loadstone to the brave and free,
And where, in bygone days, I won renown,
My vision fondly turned ; new conquests saw,
And El Dorado in Guiana found.
And when my importunity prevailed,
They let me forth, unpardoned, to pursue
My noble quest ; but sanguine of success
I had no fear ; freedom, all I craved,
To follow whither fate and fortune led
Was mine.   My honour and my life at stake,
And animated by the deepest faith
Success would crown my long projected scheme,
In this great venture I embarked my all,
Myself, my son, and all my worldly wealth,
And that brave friend, the faithful to the last.
So great the prize, so strong and firm my faith
That we the prize should win.   But treason black
And leprous ere we sailed against us worked.
I held the king's commission for the task,
Yet shamefully the king my cause betrayed,
And to the wily Gondomar revealed
Each point and tittle of my laboured plan.
Thus ruin and disaster followed us,
And met us everywhere.   My son was slain ;
Brave Captain Kemis fell by his own hand ;
The crews were mutinous, and rat-like told

Of ruin ev'n before the ruin came.
Thus sonless, friendless, fortuneless, bereft
Of hope in any power on earth, my heart
And brain alike by anguish broken down,
And knowing for the first time in my life
What sorrow truly means, I back returned,
The shattered carcase of a wretched soul.
But, O my darling Bess, my sinless wife,
My greatest sorrow is to think of thine !

Again betrayed, again cast in the Tower,
The old vile sentence was revived ; and I,
Once set at liberty though by the king,
Was still a doomed man in the eyes of law ;
And on that shameful verdict now must die.
All efforts proving vain to save my life.
Vain all petitions, prayers, my former deeds,
My toils and sufferings for my country's good.
No touch of pity ever moved the king ;
Inexorable to all appeals he proved
Deaf to the sense of honour as of shame,
For Spain was thirsting for my blood, and Spain
Was lord of England's ruler, heart and soul ;
And I shall die a sacrifice to Spain.

One triumph still is mine. I will not quail,
Nor show a sign of fear ; but all shall see
How well an English gentleman can die.

A nobler death no hero ever died.
For having none to reverence or fear
Except the King of kings, he died as one
In whose brave heart death can no terrors raise.
With steadfast step, and aspect bright and clear,
He took his last brave walk—the walk to death.
The admiration won of all who saw ;
And all who saw were sadder far than he.
All joined him in his short pathetic prayer,
In which he mercy asked, and bade farewell,
At peace alike with all men and with God.
His last few presents made, he calmly said :
" And having a long journey now to make,
" I take my leave of all." The headsman asked,
" I prithee let me see the axe. Nay, nay,
Dost think I am afraid to look upon 't ? "
Then carefully along the edge he felt,
And turning to the sheriff, smiling said,
" This medicine is sharp, but it will prove
For all diseases the physician." Then
The executioner forgiveness craved ;
Which freely was bestowed. " How will you lie ? "
The headsman asked. " So that the heart be right,
It matters nothing which way lies the head."

With these brave words the fatal blow was struck.
And one more noble soul was lost to earth.

SIR JOHN ELIOT.

DIED IN THE TOWER, *November* 27, 1632.

My England ! what a glorious roll is thine
Of great, heroic, noble, god-like men !
Since first recording annals thou couldst boast,
Ev'n till to-day, the race has never ceased.
From out the distant past they speak to us,
Though dead, they speak, inspiring strength and
    hope ;
Still making clear the path that we should tread,
To prove but worthy of such sires. And now
No Englishman deserves that honoured name
Whose heart does not with exultation beat,
Recalling Eliot's life and death. For us
He stood in danger's breach, braved tyrant power,
And waged incessant war with tongue and pen
'Gainst tyranny and wrong. For us that voice,
So eloquent and wisdom-laden, spoke,
And in the " business of posterity " [1]
Was lifted up, exposing now, and now
Denouncing those who from the vantage ground
Of place and power, with cunning and with force,

---

[1] Negotium Posterorum.

Still sought our rights and freedom to destroy ;
To overthrow the victories of the past ;
To quench the lamp our fathers' hands had lit ;
To violate the laws their blood had won,
For our security and honour of the land ;
Our glorious and hard-won liberties to blast ;
And to transform this free, self-governed realm
Into a land for lawless despotism,
Unlimited prerogative and power—
The king sole lord of all.
               This to prevent
Did Eliot and his noble compeers strive.
For this a rock amid the surging waves
Which fiercely dashed around, he firmly stood.
His passionate love of freedom and of right,
Still proving incorruptible alike
To blandishment and bribe.   He fought the fight,
And, conscious of the risk, the peril dared,
And in the forefront of assailants stood,
The inspiring word to say, the road to show,
And mark the glorious end to be attained ;
To save his country, and secure her rights,
And thus the patriot's reward to win—
Imprisonment and death.
              O noble soul
With noble body graced !   We see him now,

Through the thick veil of intervening years,
A guiding-star to all who love the light.
Again we hear that all-persuasive voice,
Which listening Senates heard in silent awe,
In wild excitement, or, by sorrow moved,
With sympathetic tears, as sadly he
Unfolded all the perils of the time ;
The violations of their sacred laws ;
Infractions of their liberties and rights ;
The shames inflicted on the Commonwealth ;
Her glory tarnished, and her strength impaired ;
Religion, and the teachings of God's Word
Abused, and sacrilegiously employed
To bind the conscience, to pervert the truth,
And sanctify injustice in men's eyes.
The people by illegal taxes pilled,
And by oppressions and exactions wrought
To misery and despair.   Thus clause by clause
The terrible indictment was unrolled
Against the many tyrannies and wrongs
Of lawless men clothed with unbridled power ;
Then showed from history and the glorious past,
How in this land the truth was ever found
That Parliaments and Freedom were conjoined ;
That when the king his lawful council loved,
The monarch o'er a happy kingdom reigned,

A people prosperous, contented, blessed.
And all who heard the story made a vow
To save alike their country and their king.
   To save their king! The king would not be
      saved.
For with that strange perversity which marks
The weak and vacillating mind, his words
And deeds no fitting correspondence bore ;
Was most resolved when most he should have
      bowed,
And bent at times when firmness had been wise.
His only aim to swell the royal power,
And raise prerogative above the law.
And for this end he paltered so with truth,
That truth and falsehood their distinctions lost,
Were equally as useful servants used
Against the nation's liberties and laws.
For this so oft he pledged the royal word
And ne'er redeemed the pawn, that soon it grew
A thing received with mockery and scorn by all,
The solemn prelude to some new deceit,
Involving some new danger to the state.
Thus by his own perverted nature led,
By evil counsels swayed, which, courtier-like,
But worked in harmony with his desires,
And made him deaf to all his people's cries :

Deaf to their wrongs, their sufferings, and shames;
Deaf to the voice of wisdom and of truth ;
And to his true and sacred duties blind,
Until the awful retribution came
Which made the country red with civil blood,
When fathers sons, and sons their fathers slew,
And brothers brothers met in deadly strife,
And, by avenging Nemesis pursued,
His own blood stained the block. ~
           From all these ills
Would Eliot save the nation and the king.
His honest loyalty, and English love
Of liberty, religion, order, law,
And all the good our noble sires had won,
Him and his loyal-hearted friends inspired
To dare all risks, all penalties endure,
In their sublime endeavours to maintain
The precious legacy their fathers left ;
And unto their posterity bequeath,
Established and enlarged, the glorious trust.
Our Eliot was the leader of this band ;
His voice was ever first denouncing wrong,
And pleading for the right. The poor man's
    friend,
He strove that justice should be free to all,
Equal alike to peasant and to peer ;

And ever struck, as with the sword of God,
Against unrighteousness in place or power.
To crush the high misleaders of the king ;
To banish favouritism from the state ;
To purify the court, the church, the law ;
To make his country noble, glorious, free—
For these great purposes he boldly spoke,
And bravely dared the inexorable hate
Of all who battened on corruption ; throve
By evil actions and oppressive deeds ;
Thus he relentless persecution gained—
Imprisonment, ay, even unto death.
But such a life will gain its own reward ;
Be blessed with calm serenity and peace,
And be, ev'n as his Master's name has been,
Crowned with a people's never-dying love ;
The reverence of the wisest and the best ;
A beacon to attract, a torch to guide,
And in the world an everlasting fame.

    Adversity bowed not this noble soul,
But only served to draw his virtues forth,
And prove his faith was founded on a rock.
Or in his " palace," [1] or his " country house," [2]
His deep serenity was ne'er disturbed ;
His love of virtue, and his trust in truth

[1] The Tower.   [2] The Marshalsea.

Ne'er faltered ev'n in his darkest hour.
The sunshine radiating from his mind,
Made bright and beautiful his gloomy cell.
And peopled it with those rare spirits past,
Who sought and wrought for wisdom and for
    truth;
His world the world of memory and of books.
  By these and his pure nature fortified,
He in his trials no disturbance felt;
Although by prison walls enclosed, shut out
From all the beauty and the loveliness
In Nature's ever-changing kingdom seen,
And from the fields and flowers he loved so well.
No day too long, no night he tedious found.
He no affright from terrors, or from fears,
Or greatness of the powers opposed, received.
No outward loss or cross e'er trouble brought;
Was ne'er oppressed by melancholy, grief,
Or sadness; but continual pleasure had
And joy in the Almighty to sustain
And comfort him.   And by the influence
Of God's free grace, though poor, he was enriched;
And by His greatness and His power secured.
His all-sufficiency supplied the heart
With confidence, with boldness, and with strength,
Which no attempt could move.   He lived

On every side encompasséd with love,
And mercy, till his joy could not be told.
And though a " prisoner, he still was free :
Being without captivity of mind." [1]

These prison days their prison books produced.
In setting down his thoughts on noble themes,
His fruitful brain, which else had torpid grown
In gloomy and enforcéd solitude,
Sweet recreation found.   And this rich toil
Converted his dark cell into a place
Of glorious employment, the bright home
Of brighter fancies, which, by reason swayed,
Became for him and us the precious founts
Of profit and delight.   Just as his voice
In other days had fearlessly described
What forms the truest Monarchy of States,
So now, by wisdom guided, with his pen

---

[1] " I have not, in all these trialls that are passed, felt the least disturbance yett wth in me.   Noe daie has seem'd too long, nor night has once been tedious ; nor fears, nor terrours, nor oppos'd power or greatness, has affrighted me.   Noe outward crosses or losses have been troublesome.   Noe griefe, nor sadnesse, nor melancholie, has opprest me.   But a con- tynuall pleasure and joy in the Almightie has still comforted me.   The influence of His graces has enricht me.   *His* power, *His* greatness, has secur'd me.   His all-sufficiency has given me both a bouldness and confidence in Him, that noe attempt could move it " (Eliot to Richard Knightley).

He pictured forth the Monarchy of Man.
The principles and government on which
The individual kingdom should be based,
And man be lord and ruler of himself.
For this truth, love, and virtue are required ;
To know the proper duties to discharge ;
To conquer evil passions, and subdue
The lusts and vile corruptions of the flesh.
As in the sight of God to walk and work,
And uncomplainingly to bear the ills
Which still attend our contests for the right.
So step by step to raise the earth to heaven,
By making all our labours here divine.
And in this ruler of his Monarchy
Our artist drew the picture of himself.

"Not credulous, but confident," he lived.
The magnanimity of his true heart
Was never tainted with a craven fear.
His hope retained its brightness to the end.
The certainty that right would yet prevail,
Still kept his dauntless spirit whole and strong,
To brave and bear the worst.   He would not seek
A favour through "the back-door of the Court ; "
But on his own integrity rely,
Supported by the consciousness of right,

And by the love and mercy of his God,
To be sustained iu danger's darkest hour ;
And from the present to the future look
To justify his honesty and truth.
   The darkest hour is near.   His royal foe,
Implacable, relentless, unappeased,
Could find no pleasure while his victim lived.
A sterner jailer to the Tower was sent,
And new restraints imposed ; his friends denied ;
His letters intercepted and refused.
In darker, damper, and more gloomy cells
He now was lodged; and, though 'twas winte
      time,
Scarce fire allowed to shield him from the cold.
And thus that noble heart by royal hate,
By cruelty most subtle and refined,
Was basely done to death.
                  Was basely done to death !
The only death that tyrants can inflict.
The mortal part was rendered unto earth,
But the immortal lives for ever ; that
Can never die ; and soon his spirit proved
More fatal to his persecutor's cause
Than ev'n his life had been ; for by his name,
And by his death for liberty endured,
The people's hearts new inspiration gained,

Their arms fresh strength, their swords a keener
    edge,
When once again the battle was renewed,
Which brought the treacherous monarch to his
    doom.

JOHN HAMPDEN.

DIED *June* 24, 1643.

A country's crises test a country's strength :
Through great events great men are recognized ;
Their greatness being measured by the power
With which they animate a people's hopes
And wisely lead them through the perilous paths
To victory and safety ; and this land,
This England, richly dowered and sweetly graced,
Encompassed by the all-protecting sea,
And consecrated from her very birth
To be the home of Freedom, and a light
To all the struggling nations of the world.
Through many glorious contests she has passed,
And never lacked her God-appointed men
To dare, to suffer, and to win the palm.
    In England's darkest days, when foolish Charles
Her hard-won freedom laboured to destroy,
And broke her sacred and most cherished laws ;
With high and haughty insolence suppressed
Her people's ancient Parliament, and sought
To tax and govern by his will alone :
When Strafford strove to arm him with the sword,
And Laud had made the Church his willing tool,

And her once fair Protestant body clothed
In Popery's cast-off finery and pomp,
And all who would not to the idol bow
With fiercest persecution were assailed,
Arrested, mutilated, fined ;
In loathsome prisons cast to rot and die—
In that dark hour a noble host arose,
Filled with a holy zeal for truth and right ;
With hearts devoted to their country's weal,
Her liberties, religion, and her laws :
Prepared the greatest trials to endure,
To save the land and faith dear to their hearts,
And worthy of the sacrifice of self,
Her ancient fame and freedom to maintain.
Of this heroic band, John Hampden's place
Is with the purest, noblest, wisest, best.
    When Charles, in violation of the laws,
Which he had sworn to honour and observe,
Sought by the exercise of his sole will
To tax the people, and their rights destroy,
The inextinguishable spirit rose,
The love of freedom which can never die
And loyal hearts a firm resistance showed ;
A glorious band of patriotic souls,
With Hampden at their head, refused the tax.
Denied the right of kings in this free land

To levy taxes, or revenue raise,
Save in the old and well-established way,
In freely-chosen Parliaments decreed :
He braved the King, and trusted to the law
In this extremity to guard the right;
But judges, pusillanimous, corrupt,
Obsequious to the royal will,
The sacred cause of justice then betrayed,
And making law subservient to power,
Unrighteous judgment gave.

                Still undismayed,
With heart which had no fear but fear of God,
He kept the upward path ; strove for the right,
With ever-deepening faith it must prevail,
And all opposing forces overcome.
And when the growing tyranny compelled
Appeal to the arbitrament of war,
In " liberty's athletic habit " [1] clad,
He drew his sword upon the people's side ;
And in the field, as in the Senate, proved
A soldier worthy of the sacred cause.
From no ambitious aim, no selfish end,
No thirst for personal aggrandisement,
No weak desire of popular applause,
But from the highest, holiest motives, he,

              [1] Algernon Sidney.

With sad resolve, and solemn consciousness
Of all the ills which from that strife would flow,
Had fixed his course, and never turned aside.
For seer-like he beyond the present looked,
And saw his high ideal realized.
The people happy, prosperous, and free,
Their freedom safe, and sanctified by law :
The king's prerogative and powers restrained,
And made subservient to the common good :
The Church reformed and purified, her rites
And services from superstition cleansed ;
Pluralities and simony suppressed ;
Her offices discharged by pious men ;
And liberty of conscience gained for all.
Thus the whole body politic would be,
Ev'n like a man with every organ sound,
Who truly lives, yet scarcely feels he lives,
So undisturbed his life's unconscious flow.

   For this his sword was drawn.   But all too soon
For England's welfare came the fatal day,
And all too soon was fired the fatal shot
Which reft the country of a hero's life,
And filled her heart with grief.   On Chalgrove
    Field—
Made famous by that deed for evermore—
When at the head of his assailing troops,

He met his death.   We can recall the scene,
The sad pathetic scene so oft described.
With head bowed down, hands on his horse's neck,
He left the field before the fight was done ;
" A thing he ne'er before was known to do,"
And faintingly and slowly rode to Thame.
Was there received by sad and loving friends,
Who nursed the dying man with pious care,
Assuaged the sufferings which they could not heal.
Six days he lingered on in cruel pains,
All patiently and without murmur borne.
Then with a prayer that God this realm would
        bless,
The enemies of freedom would confound,
The king from evil councillors withdraw,
And him and them from wicked courses turn,
And in His mercy would the country save—   ·
His noble spirit passed to blissful rest.
    With manners gentle, courteous, refined,
A temper resolute and firm, a will
Inflexible in striving for the right,
Were happily united ; and his mind
Stored richly with the wisdom of the past,
Drew inspiration from the Word of God,
And thus immutably was fortified
Against the thick temptations of the world.

And wise in counsel, he was brave in war,
A pattern and example unto all.
A perfect English gentleman he lived,
A perfect English gentleman he died :
A noble life crowned by a noble death ;
He in the ranks of Freedom's martyrs holds
A lofty place ; and in these later days
Men inspiration draw from Hampden's name.

WILLIAM, LORD RUSSELL.

BEHEADED, *July* 21, 1683.

Few years had passed since England, mad with
    hope,
The Second Charles had to the throne recalled.
The splendid triumphs of the Commonwealth
Were cast into the mire. The country's name,
Which Cromwell's mighty and far-reaching rule
Had made the admiration of the world,
Was now a thing of mockery and scorn.
The smallest powers in Europe held her cheap,
Prized not her favours, and feared not her wrath.
The greatest played with her for their own ends.
And she whose voice beyond the Alps was heard,
And made the bloody tyrant stay his hand,
Wet with the blood by persecution shed,
Was now the friend of tyranny and wrong.
She who had firmly curbed aspiring France,
And made her king and statesmen lowly bend,
Was now her slave ; the king a bondman, bought
By foreign gold his country to betray,
And sap her liberty, religion, laws,
And by base means still baser ends attain.
The Dutch, who trembled at the name of Blake,

Now rode triumphant in the narrow seas,
And with the broom symbolic swept the Thames ;
The nation's degradation and her shame.
Corruption found a home in every place,
The Church, the Senate, and the judgment seat;
Dishonourable honours crowning vice and sin.
Profligacy, naked but not ashamed,
With bold, unblushing forehead braved the world,
Deriding public shame and private scorn,
And desecrating sweet domestic life ;
While base ambition, mean venality,
And treacherous hypocrisy combined,
Had made the king a traitor to his oath,
A vassal unto France, the direst foe
Of his own land, and all she prized the most.
   In this her darkest hour true men were found
To struggle for the right.   A few beheld
The sad declension of their native land,
And bravely strove to check the downward course.
They saw what should have been her source of
      strength,
The very fount of justice, truth, and honour,
Perverted to a sluice whence issued forth
The fetid waters of disease and death.
Their shameless king a double treason planned
At home gave promise of an earnest war,

To lure from Parliament a large supply,
And as the price of peace still larger sums
From France's crafty king as alms he begged,
His country to oppress, to raise his power
Alike above the Parliaments and laws ;
The nation-hated Papacy restore,
And o'er free England reign a despot king.
An act more scandalous, dishonourable,
And base, no annals yet record.
               These deeds
The gentle-hearted Russell deeply stirred ;
While sacred indignation filled his soul
Beholding thus the monarch's shameless shame,
The perils freedom and religion ran
By foreign and domestic foes assailed,
Their sworn protector deadliest of them all.
The lineal successor to the throne,
A zealous son of Rome, the slave of priests,
And pledged their domination to restore
And lay the kingdom prostrate to the Pope.
  Against the triumph of this deadly wrong
Lord Russell strove.   With quiet fortitude
And never-swerving mind he held his course,
And venerating Parliaments—the founts
And guardians of our liberties and laws—
Through Parliament he sought to gain his ends ;

And by the ancient council of the realm
Declare no Papist should in England reign.
He knew the evils which we had to dread;
From such a scourge his country he would save.
    But for the time he failed.   The evil powers
'A' temporary triumph had secured,
And crushed their rivals with a bloody hand.
Relentless and enraged they hurried on,
Flushed with success; not dreaming of the hour
Of retribution stern and terrible,
Which every cruel act but hastened on.
The wisest, and the bravest, and the best
Of England's sons were seized, and made the prey
Of lawless law and uncontrolled revenge.
    And of these victims Russell was the first.
On charges false, and perjured evidence,
By shameless oaths of traitors and of spies,
A jury prejudiced, a judge corrupt,
The noble patriot was condemned to death.
Nor could the prayers of his heroic wife—
The pattern and example of her sex—
Inspired by deathless love, the country save
From this judicial murder's dark disgrace.
    That trial was our glory and our shame.
Our shame through the perversion of the law,
When judge became the prosecutor too,

And wrested justice to unholy ends;
When one who never sought to kill the king,
Nor·levy war against his government,
Of both offences thus was guilty found,
And most illegally condemned to death :
Our glory that in such an evil time
Men dared the peril in defence of right,
And glorious are to all succeeding times :
By that true heroine, a noble wife,
Who through the ordeal of that fatal day
Still by his side was found with ready help,
And wise advice to aid him in his need.
O noble soul, that worthy act of thine,
Joined to the record of thy blameless life,
For him and thee has won immortal fame,
And through all ages men will sing thy praise,
His death a murder call.
     Serene and calm
He waited his last hour. His faith in God,
And in the sure redemption wrought by Christ,
Made death the entrance to eternal life,
A thing for joy, not fear. And he rejoiced
That in possession of his wonted strength,
His faculties not weakened by disease,
His intellect undimmed, still clear and bright,
He cheerfully could say farewell to life ;

And all his foes and all who had conspired,
Or high or low, to bring him to the block,
He could forgive with an unclouded mind.
And in this blessèd mood his days were spent.
His noble wife, with her courageous love,
Sustaining and consoling to the last,
The sanctifying angel of the prison.
And now, all the heartrending farewells said,
The last embrace and sacred kisses given,
He felt the "bitterness of death was past,"
And all the rest was happiness and bliss.

    Of this great tragedy one scene remains,
The headsman and the axe.   Refreshed by sleep,
As sound as that which guileless childhood knows,
A message to his wife that all was well;
His watch to Burnet promised, with the words—
"I've done with time; eternity begins;"
With firm, unfaltering step he reached the coach,
And singing to himself a holy psalm,
"Which soon," he said, "I shall much better
    sing,"
He stood beside the block; there knelt and prayed;
With modest firmness, countenance unchanged,
No sign of fear, he calmly laid him down,
And yielding·thus his body to the earth,
He gave his soul to God.

One hero more
Of that long list our famous England boasts,
Sealed with his blood his hatred of all wrong;
His love of liberty, his crowning hope
To make his nation glorious and free !

ALGERNON SIDNEY.

BEHEADED, *December* 7, 1683.

O God-like Freedom ! from my earliest years
My soul has worshipped thee.   My infant tongue
Was taught to feebly syllable thy praise.
My boyhood's days were passed in learning all
The glorious record of thy bright career.
How men inspired by thee have done and dared ;
How nations, by thy voice invoked, arose,
Thy banner spread, and struck the tyrant down,
And lived thenceforth on freedom's sun-lit heights.
My youthful blood with wildest rapture thrilled,
My heart with glowing aspirations burned,
As on the ever-living classic page,
The glorious tale of Greece and Rome, I read,
Until imagination could recall,
As pictured visibly before my eyes,
Those mighty nations struggling to be free ;
Bequeathing to the world the priceless truths
That liberty alone can make a land
Great, worthy of the favour of the gods—
That misery, decay and death will come
When but one man shall grasp the sovran rule
And be a tyrant o'er a realm of slaves.

I studied next the story of my land,
My native land ; more precious to my heart
Than is the life-blood flowing through these veins,
And dearer far to me than is the life
Which in her honour freely I lay down.
My spirit rose at every word and deed
By patriot and by martyr said and done,
In freedom's holy cause from earliest times
Ev'n to the present day.   I traced her growth
Through all the wondrous changes of the past ;
How, step by step, she from the lowest depths
Of serfdom and of bondage grandly rose
And rent her chains asunder ; breaking down
The iron barriers tyranny had raised
To stay her upward march—but raised in vain.
In vain the sword, the prison, and the stake ;
Her soaring spirit would not be repressed,   ·
But waxed the stronger after each defeat,
Until victoriously the road was cleared
For others marching on the blood-stained track,
Still greater triumphs to attain.   And now
The peer united with the peasant rose
To check despotic kings ; and now the king
Upon the people called to overcome
The insolent aggressions of the peers.
Fierce were the contests, for the prize was great.

And scarce a spot in England can be found,
Which is not more than sacred from the blood
Of her own sons contending for the right—
The right to live as freemen or to die.
And thus through centuries of changeful strife
The never-doubtful war of right and wrong
Successfully was waged; till England saw
Her Parliaments still strong and stronger grow,
Asserting the supremacy of law
To fix and bind prerogative of kings.

But never in the contests of the past
Has such a blow for liberty been struck,
As in these latter days. For ne'er before,
By an astonished and admiring world,
Was spectacle so grand and solemn seen :
A king arraigned before the nation's bar,
For violations of his sacred oath,
For ruthless shedding of his people's blood,
For treasons manifold against the State ;
To public trial brought and guilty found,
And doomed to death !
                      And with the sword and tongue,
In Parliament and in the field alike
I bore my portion in the glorious fight,
But only fought for liberty in both.
For when another tyranny arose

My voice was lifted up against the wrong,
Opposing Cromwell as I Charles opposed:
For never to a tyrant would I yield,
Whether he were Protector called, or King.
   Then from my home an exile I retired;
For in my country I could only live
By means far worse than would be dying there.
To see a people wholly sacrificed;
For one man's profit and his pleasure used;
His glory but their shame, his weal their woe;
A land, if liberty had been preserved,
Most famous and most glorious in the world,
But now more miserable and wretched made
By that great height of glory whence she fell.
For this, in foreign lands, with strangers I,
Alone, companionless, and friendless dwelt.
Where Lambert, Vane, and Haselrigge could not
In safety live, I could not live at all;
For life is worthless to a noble mind,
That lives not by just means just ends to serve.
If for his people's good the king would rule,
Then none more loyally the king would serve;
But while by tyranny his course is marked,
His enemy I am in heart and soul.[1]

[1] See Sidney's letter to his friend, giving reasons for not returning to England.

At last, with pardon promised, I returned,
And breathed in hope my native air again.
Still to my heart the Good Old Cause was dear,
And liberty the end for which I strove,
Shamed by the sycophantic spirit shown ;
The flagrant profligacy blazed abroad ;
The ribald treatment of all sacred things ;
High places purchased by a harlot's smile ;
The people's treasures spent in wicked waste ;
The Church turned to a servile instrument
To sanctify oppression, fraud, and wrong ;
The founts of life corrupted and made foul,
Till manly strength seemed vanished from the land ;
And virtue, once triumphant, lay concealed
In lowly homes, or fired a noble few
The soul-destroying flood to stem.
                                  But these
Were from the grovelling herd soon singled out,
The patriot's crown of suffering to bear.
For, by suspicion marked, the guilty powers
In persecution their own safety sought ;
Sham plots concocted, and false charges made,
The mockery of trials held, at which,
With juries packed, and judges venal, sold
Before they took their seats, to wrest the law,
All justice to refuse, defence deny,

But resolute to shed their victims' blood ;
For they must die, or else the plot would die.
For this was spotless Russell made to bleed ;
For this I follow in his glorious path,
The self-same road unto the self-same end,
And for the self-same cause.

                  A nobler death
No honourable man need wish to die.
For still in all the ages of the world
Men gladly suffered for their country's good.
And never yet with deeper peace and joy,
With higher and with further-reaching hopes,
Did one lay down his life in freedom's cause
Than I shall lay down mine to-morrow morn.
   Ah, pleasantly do I remember now,
My shameful trial o'er, and sentence passed,
The partial judge, assuming I had shown
A touch of passion in my final words,
Blushed not to pray God would my temper fit
For th' other world, so all unmeet for this.
But then, as now, my pulses calmly beat,
My temper no disorder felt.   For I
Have far too often looked on death to fear.
He never moved me yet, and will not now.
Serene and undisturbed, as I to-night
Shall seek for sleep, the " death of each day's life,"

So I shall lay my head upon the block,
Appealing to the great Eternal Judge,
Who judges not as man.
                              O sovran Judge,
These practices forgive ! Avert the ills
That else will on this misruled nation fall.
Lord, sanctify my sufferings unto me.
And though to idols I am sacrificed,
Let not idolatry reign in the land.
The people bless and save.   Thy cause defend.
And all defending Thy great cause, O Lord !
Stir up the faint, the willing hearts direct,
The waverers confirm, and fill them all
With wisdom, and integrity, and trust.
And order all things so that all things still
Unto Thy glory may rebound.   Oh, grant
That for Thy mercies glorifying Thee
I too may die !   My thanks and praise I give
For Thy permission to be singled out
A witness for Thy truth, for that Old Cause,
To which from youth my heart and soul were
        pledged,
Which Thou so wonderfully hast approved.
For this I've lived, and for this cause I die.
Accept the willing sacrifice, O Lord ! [1]

[1] See Sidney's last address to " Men, Brethren and
Fathers ; Friends, Countrymen, and Strangers ! "

APRIL 23RD, 1864.

O gentle-hearted Shakspere, unto thee
  My faltering tongue its loyal praise would sing !
I know how all unworthy it must be,
  For who to thee can fitting tribute bring ?
The tongues of all the nations join in vain
To lay upon thy shrine a worthy strain.

Yet as a little child with prattling tongue
  His sire's unfathomable wisdom boasts,
And in his lisping treble, pipes his song
  Of praise, amid his wond'ring school-boy hosts :
So I in trembling accents sing of thine,
Our poet, myriad-minded and divine.

And as 'tis love inspires his childish praise,
  So love wins for his words acceptance meet ;
Such pure unquestioning faith is sure to raise
  A joy in every heart's responsive beat :
So deepest love, for these weak words may gain
A grace denied to more ambitious strain.

How often 'neath that sacred roof I've stood
  In which thy gentle eyes first saw the light !

Where o'er thy earliest fancies thou didst brood,
   And welcome childhood's visions with delight.
And in the mind's eye there have yearned to see
Some picture of the life then lived by thee.

And oft along the willow-haunted banks
   Of thy belovéd stream my feet have strayed,
And oh ! how often have I given thanks,
    That mid such scenes thy earliest songs were
      made !
Each grassy isle, each flower, and weed, and tree,
A thing of beauty was and joy to thee.

And each in thy immortal song has won
   Perennial bloom that winter cannot kill ;
For Shakspere's flowers, shone on by Shakpere's
    sun,
   We gather all the year, and when we will.
And watching here the gentle Avon's flow,
He saw them first in nature's purest glow.

And all the lovely scenes thy home around,
   Where'er I felt that thou in sooth hadst been,
My pilgrim feet have sought as sacred ground ;
   And every spot on which thy eyes serene

May erst have gazed, to me henceforth became
Connected with thy life, and fame, and name.

But mostly where thy first-love days were passed,
    With her—whatever foolish critics say—
Who was thy first, thy life-love, and thy last,
    My steps have haunted, thinking of the day,
When 'neath the hawthorn, or the elm-tree shade
Thy words of love first won the happy maid.

Ah me ! what love-words fell from thy sweet tongue !
    So honey-freighted woman's heart to gain !
Man never listened yet to siren's song,
    So witching sweet as was thy loving strain.
And near thy love-haunts I would fondly stray
And dream of thee beneath the blind boy's sway.

Then follow thee amid the haunts of men,
    Where thy young strength won early victory ;
Where loving Spenser and proud-hearted Ben,
    And all the sons of song acknowledged thee
Their lord and king ! yet loved thee none the less,
So all-enthralling was thy gentleness.

Our multiform humanity to thee
    Was as an open book ; thy piercing eye

Each spring of action, motive-cause could see;
   And e'en its inmost secrets could descry.
No passion housing in the human heart,
But to interpret it thou hadst the art.

O master mind! full well they knew thy sway!
   But raise thy wand and each in turn appears
In willing haste thy mandate to obey.
   Joy, sorrow, love, hate, laughter, mirth, and tears,
Hope, and despair—whate'er belongs to men
All lay within thy far-extending ken.

And on our greatness thou wouldst proudly dwell;
   And on our meanness look with pitying eye;
Since every form of life thou knew'st full well,
   And had with all a poet's sympathy.
No human action was too great or small,
But thy large catholic heart embraced them all.

And thou wast dowered with immortal speech;
   Thy people live for us; will live for aye:
And sires unborn will unborn children teach
   How fitting homage for thy works to pay.
For long as men exist, and worlds shall be,
We may not hope a greater soul than thee.

And now once more beside thy tomb I stand,
  And watch the glory of thy mighty brow.
And through this some time dumb, but grateful land
  Are myriads seeking how they best may show,
Upon this ever memorable morn,
Their gratitude that thou wast English born.

Three hundred years ago a little child,
  Unconscious in thy nurse's arms wast thou.
And now upon this April morning mild
  The nations onward to thy birth-place flow,
And own God gives no blessing to this earth
Can equal a true poet in its worth.

How grand the power to win a nation's love;
  How grand to prove the poet of thy race; .
How grand to see the people freely move
  And bring their tribute to thy resting-place.
The free heart-offering of their love and praise—
So gloriously perennial are thy bays.

Now comes the blaze of pomp; the joyous cry
  Of joyous thousands; peals of bells; the show;
The flaunting banners, and the pageantry;
  The long, long-drawn procession, and the glow

Of happy faces, gathered to proclaim
How dear to them their poet's deathless fame !

And I in silence may not pass the day.
　The strain is feeble, but the theme is great.
A nation keeping one bright holiday
　Because three hundred years ago kind fate
Ordained that on this thrice, thrice happy morn,
On Avon's bank our poet should be born.

And so with all the world my voice I raise ;
　And mingle with their shouts my tremulous
　　sound.
I cannot pay my debt ; nor hope to praise
　In strains befitting thee whose name I sound.
But as my tribute these poor words of mine,
With reverence I lay upon thy shrine.

Accept it, thou all-sympathizing one !
　O'erlook its faults ; its love source only see.
Of all who honour thee, I yield to none
　In love, in heart-felt reverence to thee.
And gentle Shakspere, let that love obtain
Acceptance for this tributary strain.

SHAKSPERE'S DAY.

Again the course of time brings round
    This ever glorious day;
And every heart on English ground
Beats high with pride and joy profound,
Remembering him whose mighty name
Is honour, splendour, wealth, and fame,
    That ne'er will pass away.

'Tis April with us once again,
    In smiles and tears arrayed.
From every tree the thrilling strain
Of amorous birds, warmed by the pain
And joy of love, breaks out in song
As musical as when along
    The Avon's banks he strayed.

And reawakened Nature now
    Has broken Winter's chain,
And wreathing flowers around her brow,
Is radiant with beauty's glow;
While Hope before her steps appears,
And Gladness welcomes her with cheers,
    Joy follows in her train.

She smiles, and lo ! the vale and hill,
    The hedge-side and the lea,
Do Flora's sweetest children fill
With fragrance and with beauty, till
The heart of man bounds with delight,
Each sense rejoicing at the sight
    Of earth's deep ecstasy.

And in this month, and on this morn,
    In England's fairest shire,
Was human-nature's poet born,
All coming ages to adorn :
The man of men, the lord of song,
The king of that immortal throng
    Endowed with vatic fire.

For such a birth, oh ! fitting time,
    The Spring-time of the year !
When life renews her early prime,
In graceful beauty, strength sublime,
In bud and blade, in song and flowers,
In sun-illuminated showers,
    Bids all her wealth appear.

To fitting time was fitting place
    By nature pre-ordained;
Of freedom's land, of English race,
Of Saxon lineage, Saxon face,
And speaking too the Saxon tongue,
Meet for the universal song
    That from his lips he rained.

Right in the heart of this great land,
    God-chosen, fair, and free,
Where matchless sylvan scenes seem planned
The poet's praises to command :
Where Avon's willow-shaded stream,
Whose flower-clad isles and lilies gleam
    A pleasure but to see :

'Twas here our Shakspere saw the light,
    Fit place and season too ;
Here did his youthful mind delight
To ramble 'mid these meadows bright,
And all those wondrous secrets gain
That made the world-wide poet's strain
    To live all ages through.

F

For he and nature were at one ;
    On him she laid her hand :
His heart with hers in unison
Beat musically ; and he won
The grace she only can bestow
On open souls that truly know
    The love of her command.

And in this April time once more
    The world forgets its care,
And hails the glorious day that bore
So rich a treasure to our door.
Again all lands with joy divine
In reverential love combine
    This festival to share.

O England, thus supremely blest,
    With such a dower endowed ;
Lift up thy voice 'bove all the rest ;
Rejoice with still-increasing zest ;
And ever welcome in this day
With grateful song and glad huzza,
    And praises deep and loud !

PINTURICCHIO.

" He appears to have made, like Andrea del Sarto, an unfortunate marriage. Whilst he was suffering under a severe illness, his wife quitted the house with a lover, closed the door, and left the unhappy painter to die of neglect and starvation."   A. H. LAYARD.

And this then is the end of all my Art !
My life, so fraught with glory, ends in this !
Bound, impotent, unaided, here I lie,
A prey to hunger, and remorseful thoughts,
Each thought more bitter than the hunger-pang !
Why did I marry ?   Oh, my God ! the fool
I was to suffer divorce from my Art,
And wed a woman, giving her the power
To curse me ; to destroy me—leave me thus ! .

And yet how beautiful she was !   I know—
For I have seen the vulgar gaze with awe ;
Have seen the flush of rapture in the eye ;
Have heard th' involuntary tribute said
By men whose words are honour, glory, fame,
When looking on the work of these weak hands—
I know my warm imagination has
In moments of rapt inspiration formed

Things of ideal loveliness, to which
My faithful eye, my firm and skilful hand
With visible existence have endowed,
For men to love, to worship, and adore.
But than the fairest she is far more fair.
What tints could ever paint her glorious flesh ?
What genius fix her love-compelling smile ?
Not even my passion-guided pencil reached
The ravishing luxuriance of her hair,
Nor made immortal any grace of hers.
The subtle changes of her beauteous face,
Still varying with her ever-changeful mood,
Were seen, and loved, and lost, ere one could say,
" Behold ! how beautiful she is ! "   And I ?
O God !   I was entranced.   I looked on her
Till fascination turned me to a slave.
Her beauty held me spell-bound ; and I took
A woman's form, without a woman's soul,
Unto my heart, and called her mine.   And she,
Because the people praised me, and the men
Who rule—the wise, the rich, the lords of earth,
Endowed with love of my immortal art—
Had gathered round me, honoured me as friend,
And placed me in their council-chambers—she
From merest woman's vanity, not love,
Became my wife, and took the holy vows

She never kept—the perjured child of shame!
The beauty I had loved with heart and soul,
As only painters can—the beauty I
With wild devotion to my heart had pressed,
And placed even as a goddess in my shrine,
Proved but a venomed serpent—and it stung!

I see her now. Her matchless arm is round
Her guilty lover's neck! Her glorious head—
Crowned with the splendour of her shining hair,
In which *my* fingers lovingly have played,
Whilst I, with pride, have wondered at its mass,
And, playfully unwinding it, have showered
The thickly-waving ringlets round and round,
Until they hid her face, and neck, and breast,
She laughing—that head, so loved, so honoured
      once,
On her deluded paramour reclines.
Her eyes—those wicked, sparkling eyes—upturned,
Gaze loving on his overhanging face,
As they have gazed on mine : and on her lips,
That pouting still the sweet impression woo,
His lavish and unholy kisses fall!
And she, this beauteous evil, bears my name,
And is my wife ; and I—am starving here!

God's curse light on her ! There ! I have said
    it !
I never thought these lips would breathe a curse
On her, my beautiful ! Yet she has been
Nought but a curse to me. I see it now.
My past is all before me. What has been
I see, and see, alas ! what might have been,
But for the curse that one most lovely face
Brought with it for a dower. Oh, how I loved
That graceful piece of wickedness ! And how
I strove for wealth, for honour, and for fame,
That I might hang them all as jewels round
Her brow, and crown her Queen of them and
    me !
Men praised my works, and spoke and wrote of
    them
As things divine and beautiful. And I—
I knew they were divine and beautiful ;
For love, the love of her who seemed to me
The sum of all perfection in herself,
Was e'er the source whence inspiration came,
And gave to my Madonnas life and truth,
A mother's tenderness, a woman's grace,
And all those nameless charms which still have
    power
To gladden and to bless.

How weak I am !
I cannot call for help !   Is no one here ?
She surely has not left me thus to die !
And yet how many hours have slowly passed
Since her light foot, her soft and gentle voice
Made music in my ears !   Am I grown deaf?
I cannot hear them now.   I am not deaf.
I hear the cricket's chirp, the feet of mice.
As, undisturbed, they patter o'er the floor.
There is a dimness, also, 'bout my eyes,
And yet I see the room is void and bare,
But *her* I cannot see.   I call to mind
I heard two voices whispering at the door ;
And one was harsh and rough; and she said,
    " Hush ! "
How quick and sharp the pangs about my heart
Are growing, and how quiet all things seem !
'Tis very long since I have tasted food.
How hungry I am now.   *She* might have left
A little bread and water within reach,
For one too weak to rise.   To leave me thus !
And once she vowed she loved me.   Ah ! such
    love !

    I wonder how she feels, or will feel when
My gaunt and sorrow-stricken form, my wan

And hunger-sharpened face shall dog her steps,
And haunt her—as they will—in all she does !
Ay, at the altar, as she kneels in prayer,
My presence will the murderess attend,
And damn her with her guilt ! I need not curse :
Her memory will curse her evermore.

How still, and dark, and cold all Nature is !
I cannot see the sky ! 'Tis very dark !

ELIZABETH BARRETT BROWNING.

Come mourn with me, all who have hearts to love
 The brave, the tender, and the beautiful:
Let deepest.anguish every feeling move,
 For loss of her whose mighty mind was full
   Of holiest thought ;
   Who nobly wrought
God's richest treasure for a suffering world to cull.

Come mourn all ye whose pulses ever beat
 To hear of God-like and of glorious deeds ;
Who feel a joy divine when tongues repeat
 The tale of right triumphant ; when succeeds
   Fair Freedom's cause ;
   When rescued laws
Make tyrants tremble, like the river-shaken reeds.

Come mourn with me, all who have found delight
 In listening, rapt, to Poesy's sweet song ;
The voice is hushed whose pæan's magic might
 Thrilled through the world the curse of shame-
   less wrong,
   Whose glorious peal,
   Made Nations feel,
How God-like 'tis for man, to be both free and
   strong !

Come mourn with me ! for never, never more
   Shall those pure, passionate utterings be heard,
That fired us with such hopes, and made us soar
   Till every pulse in unison was stirred,
        And nations rose
        Against their foes,
The foes of human rights which God Himself
    conferred.

Come mourn with me the loss of one so gifted,
   Of her whose voice in richest cadences
Was for the poor and the oppressed uplifted,
   And poured its withering scorn on tyrannies.
        For aye appealing,
        With earnest feéling,
From men's base laws to the Eternal's just decrees.

Come mourn with me ! we ne'er shall hear again
   Those music-dowered lips, for whose rich song
Unnumbered hearts have yearned ! No more that
    strain
   Shall flood-like roll its sweeping torrent strong.
        No more, no more,
        'Bove evil's roar,
Shall that grand voice resound denouncing sin and
    wrong.

Come mourn with me, ye lovers fond and true!
  Who now will sing your tender hopes and fears?
Who now will give you words with which to woo?
  Who now will consecrate your joyous tears?
      That voice is mute,
      Which like a lute,
So oft has touched the heart with strains that thrilled
      it through.

Come mourn with me, ye patriots who desire
  The spread of Freedom's glorious empery;
For never more in words of scathing fire,
  Will she be heard denouncing tyranny;
      Nor with acclaim
      Of joy, proclaim
The victory of truth o'er falsehood's demon sire.

Come mourn with me, ye who the muses love;
  Who bow before their consecrated shrine;
For she will sing no more; nought now can move
  That darling of the Heliconian Nine.
      No lyric song,
      Swift, sweet, and strong;
No resonant mighty verse; no all-entrancing line.

Come mourn with me ! Ours is no common woe.
  Nations should weep whene'er a poet dies.
Too rarely such a gift does God bestow,
  Too rarely we that gift know how to prize.
        We pay with scorn,
        And oft the thorn,
Instead of laurel-crown, our loving care supplies.

Ours is no common woe ; no common loss ;
  The Queen of England's matchless singer she.
She bravely bore the Poet's crown and cross,
  And won through sorrow song's high victory.
        She bore her dower
        Of vatic power
With man's grand strength, with woman's sweet
        humility.

Come mourn with me !—And yet she is not dead !
  The songs she sung are ours : can never die.
Immortal as the soul that now has fled
  To join her peers, the white-robed bands on high.
        Her every word .
        Still strikes a chord
Within our hearts which beats responsive sympathy.

Yet o'er her grave the tears perforce will flow :
 The very flowers shed drops of sacred dew.
Oh, loved and honoured was the dust below,
 Whence all too soon the soaring spirit flew,
   In peace to rest,
   On Christ's own breast,
The source whence it on earth such inspirations
   drew.

She lives ! she lives ! And yet we weep and weep ;
 Her soul is with us, yet our hearts are sad.
We loved the flesh and blood, and fain would keep
 The human casket, with the wealth it had.
   The form and face
   We love to trace ;
We love to grasp the hand ; to hear the voice are
   glad.

And thus our heads are bowed ; our eyes are wet ;
 Our grief will not be soothed ; nor calmed our
   woe.
The glory of her works but swells regret ;
 The splendours of her legacy but show
   Our loss the more ;
   The precious store
She left, reveals how rich the source whence they
   did flow.

Our rich inheritance from her possessed
  But deepens grief; intensifies our pain.
The heart broods o'er it with a sad unrest,
  And fancies what divine unuttered strain
        Her ripening powers
        Had yet made ours :
What glorious thoughts conceived by her swift
        teeming brain.

But death our hopes with envious boast has slain.
  And sorrow's garb, and sorrow's speech alone
Express the sadness felt. We mourn again
  Our loss of joys that never can be known,
        Until we meet
        In love complete,
Her radiant spirit blest, beside th' Eternal throne !

THE EVER-PRESENT.

Go through thy life without fear, if thy days be
  cloudy or bright,
For ever-present is God, alike in the darkness or
  light.

If thy pathway be strewed with flowers, or thorns
  press into thy feet,
He can make smooth the rough, and the bitter can
  change to the sweet.

The rain and the sunshine alike His love and His
  grace bestow,
And both, O brother, are needed, ere the heart can
  strengthen and grow.

No tear can fall from the eye, not a smile illumine
  the face,
But each is a mark of love, a token of mercy and
  grace.

Joys are signs of His presence, and sorrow a part
  of His plan,
And both are beneficent teachers to mould and
  perfect man.

'Tis only when raindrops are falling, and flowers
   are wet with tears,
The colours of Iris are seen, the Bow of Promise
   appears.

And life were reft of its glory, the soul deprived of
   her gain,
If lost were splendour or gloom, the changes of
   pleasure and pain.

Welcome the storm and sunshine, be glad in the
   silence of night;
Anguish is prelude to rapture, darkness the herald
   of light.

Fear not, whatever befall thee : rejoice, O heart,
   and be strong !
Converting all sorrow to wisdom, crowning all
   anguish with song.

For over all changes we see the Unchangeable rules
   and reigns ;
And above all discords apparent are heard har-
   monious strains.

Orb unto orb utters music, orderly rolling through
    space ;
The law their motions controlling, the dewdrop
    holds in its place.

And dewdrop, and orb, and man, and whatever is
    or appears,
Are pages inscribed by His hand Who makes and
    governs the spheres.

Th' infinite beauty of calms, the terror and glory of
    storms,
The world-studded halls of space, and the still
    developing forms,

Are witnesses ever revealing the one Omnipotent
    Mind
Which still, "unhasting, unresting," will perfect the
    end designed.

In Whom we live and we move, as the Teacher of
    old maintained,
Not by the heaven of heavens, nor the depths of
    ocean contained.

March, then, through life without fear, though
   thorny the path to be trod ;
A Father is here to guide, for everywhere present
   is God.

THE SIEGE OF BRESCIA, 1239.

Twas in Italia's ancient days,
  Before she reached her prime ;
Ere Art had graced life's common ways,
  Or heard was Dante's rhyme.

But Liberty cheer'd with her smile
  The cities in that age—
Too great to fear the tyrant's guile,
  Too strong to heed his rage.

From his Sicilian kingdom came
  The Second Frederick bold,
And far and wide, with sword and flame,
  His deadly presence told.

With serried ranks of hired troops,
  He struck at Freedom's heart ;
On many a town the vulture swoops,
  Swift as the lightning's dart.

At last his mighty host appears,
  Before old Brescia's walls ;
Their presence wakes no coward fears,
  Their force no heart appals.

Day after day his engines pour
  Their charges on the town ;
They hide the sun, so thick the shower
  Of deadly missiles thrown.

Day after day, week after week,
  The siege is still maintained ;
In vain the foes for triumph seek,
  No foot of ground is gained.

By fury fired, the baffled king
  Devised a cruel plan ;
He bade them forth his prisoners bring,
  And strip them man by man.

" And thus before my rams," he cried,
  "The caitiffs firmly bind ;
And those who dare our power deride,
  Shall friends for targets find."

The ghastly freighted castles move
  Unto the walls more near ;
Oh, who dare now his valour prove?
  Who rise above his fear ?

And those who have their weapons raised
  To hurl against the foe,

Their arms restrain, for sore amazed,
 They know not where to throw

" Oh, heed us not, but do your best ! "
 The fettered Brescians cry.
" Now hurl your darts against our breast;
 For Brescia let us die !"

Oh what a loud, responsive shout,
 The glorious words receive !
The heroes through the gates rush out,
 Rejoicing, though they grieve.

Then noble Losco leads the way,
 Although before his eyes
His son is bound to be the prey :
 By the first stroke he dies.

With arrows, and with torches bright,
 With fire, and sword, and lance,
Against the tyrant's cruel might
 The citizens advance.

And deadly was the conflict now;
 Death garnered well his prey;
And dark was Frederick's face and brow,
 As he beheld the fray.

He saw his bravest fall before
  The strong arm of the free ;
In vain to front his banner bore,
  His vanquished forces flee.

Then rose the grateful shout to heaven,
  The long-borne siege is raised ;
And earnest thanks to God are given,
  His boundless mercies praised.

Through all Italia's cities fair
  The glorious tidings spread ;
And joyous shoutings rend the air,
  And joyous tears are shed.

And Brescia's gallant sons are blessed
  By old and young alike ;
The men who scorned to be oppressed,
  Who dared the tyrant strike.

Though ages since that siege have passed,
  Undimmed is still its glory !
Still Freedom-loving hearts beat fast
  At Brescia's noble story.

THE MERRY LITTLE MOUNTAIN STREAM.

From cavernous darkness I burst into light,
Musical, sparkling, and merry, and bright,
Increasing in strength and in speed as I flow
To the flowery valley there blooming below;
'Midst the heather and bracken I hurry along,
Leaping, and rippling, and singing my song;
O'er my rock-bouldered bed I joyously fly,
For a merry little mountain stream am I !

Through the bright sunny valley I speed on my
    way,
Though the flowers with kisses my waters would
    stay;
Their beauty and fragrance they on me bestow
As I smile on their petals and onward I flow;
And the brightest of flowers are those in whose face
I have looked with delight, and blessed with my
    grace,
And I ripple with pride as I bid them good-bye,
For a merry little mountain stream am I !

Through thick copses unseen I prattle along,
My whereabouts told by my joy-giving song;

And I smile in my heart as I secretly flow
At the beauties unnumbered that shelter me so;
And I laugh out a rich mellow peal of delight
As I burst from the flower-starred splendour of
    night,
And bounding along greet the open blue sky,
For a merry little mountain stream am I !

But my chiefest delight as I haste to the sea,
Is the bright little journey I run through the lea,
For there on my banks at each soft twilight hour,
Come the young-hearted lovers with bliss for their
    dower,
And with arms interlaced they look on as I flow,
Their rapture revealed in the cheek's sunny glow,
And I list to each tale, and repeat every sigh,
For a merry little mountain stream am I !

Oh my life is a round of pleasure and song;
My days are passed blithely the flowers among;
And music and laughter I scatter about,
And the children reply with a light-hearted shout;
And joyous and jocund, unfettered and free,
I bound on and on till I am lost in the sea;
Absorbed in whose bosom I happily lie,
For a merry little mountain stream am I !

THE CUCKOO.

Earth is never weary
  Of thy song, sweet bird !
Gone is winter dreary
  When thy voice is heard.
Then it tells of sun and flowers,
April's ever welcome showers.

Though thy notes ne'er vary,
  Still the same old two,
Pleasant, sweet, and airy,
  Ringing the dales through ;
Sweeter never meet the ear
From the song-birds of the year.

With thy song, what visions,
  Splendour-crowned arise !
Flower-strewn Elysians
  Glad both heart and eyes :
Full of beauty, full of grace,
Spirit-haunted every place.

Rambles through the heather,
  Fern, and gorse, and brake ;

Sunny walks together
  Through the fields we take ;
Rippling streamlets, sweetly low,
Murmur as we breathe our vow.

All the summer's glory
  Doth thy song foreshadow ;
Love's unchanging story,
  Told in lane and meadow ;
Blending Nature's symphony,
With the heart's deep melody.

Pictures bright of children,
  Gaily plucking flowers,
Without let or hindering
  From forbidding powers.
Over lawn, and lane, and lea,
On they skip right merrily.

Laughter sweet as singing—
  Sweet bright bird as thine—
Through the woods are ringing
  From lips infantine ;
Sounds to make the angels smile,
Free from sorrow, free from guile.

Buttercups and daisies
  At thy coming rise;
Mutely swell thy praises
  With their golden eyes :
Golden eyes of beauty, whence
Beams their child-like innocence.

As I lie and listen
  To thy pleasant song,
Morning dew-drops glisten
  From the flowery throng—
Beauties redolent of grace
Look up smiling in my face.

Bird of birds, for ever
  Thou hast been a joy !
Men forget thee never ;
  Nothing can destroy
All the glowing prophecy
That in Spring-time wells from thee.

THE LOVE-CHEAT.

I.

She loved me, she said, and she swore it ;
  She swore it a thousand times :
She treasured my letters like jewels ;
  She learned and repeated my rhymes.

II.

And numberless tokens she gave me ;
  Her kisses were many and sweet ;
And I thought her an angel from heaven
  While she was but a womanly cheat.

III.

She robbed me of rest and of comfort,
  And gave me bright hopes in return ;
And now, by the fireside lonely,
  Her letters I smilingly burn.

IV.

For loud are the marriage bells pealing :
  The priest, too, is blessing the bride ;
And she leans on the arm of another,
  Who once was my love and my pride.

V.

Ah, well ! let her live and be married :
  Her letters are burnt, and I see
'Tis better be rid of such tokens,
  And keep the heart healthy and free.

POETRY.

———

When sorrow fills the heart with gloom
  And casts a veil o'er earth and sky,
What can restore life's healthy bloom
  Like Poetry ?

When sickness makes the pulse decline,
  And on a bed of pain we lie ;
A tonic and an anodyne
  Is Poetry.

When presses most the fight for life,
  And snarls the wolf of poverty ;
What gives such courage for the strife,
  As Poetry ?

When joy thrills through heart, blood, and brain,
  And but to live is ecstasy,
The crowning, celebrating strain
  Is Poetry.

When we unto the goal have pressed,
  And won the wreath of victory,
Our joy can only be expressed
  In Poetry.

But oh ! when love, like new-made wine,
   Makes glad the heart, and bright the eye,
Then first we learn how all divine
   Is Poetry.

And when we reach the crowning bliss
   Breathed in the soft and sweet reply,
The sealing, consecrating kiss
   Is Poetry.

The voice of love, the bridal song,
   The plaint of woe, joy's pœan cry,
In every clime, in every tongue,
   Is Poetry.

In every mood and change of life,
   When doubt is strong, or faith is high,
Nought soothes our peace, or cheers our strife,
   Like Poetry.

THE WOOING TIME OF LIFE.

Oh, the wooing time of life!
The sweet wooing time of life!
When all the year is spring,
And hearts unbidden sing,
And murmur to themselves like a tree-o'ershaded
      brook,
That with forget-me-nots is strewed,
And sweetly gliding through a wood
Ripples softly night and day,
While sun or moon-beams o'er it play;
And the soul is filled with bliss by a smile or a look.

Oh, the wooing time of life!
The sweet wooing time of life!
When every charm and grace
Meet in one belovéd face,
And crown the world with beauty, with splendour,
      and with worth;
When all is good and bright
That meets the raptured sight;
When love its fountain fills
In the beating heart that thrills
With the sense that once again there is Paradise on
      earth.

Oh, the wooing time of life!
The sweet wooing time of life!
When the present is delight,
And the future, looming bright,
Sheds a rich prophetic halo round every passing day;
When the birds in wood and grove
Sing for ever of their love;
When the earth is sweet with flowers,
And the golden wingéd hours,
Pleasure unalloyed bestowing, flee joyously away!

Oh, the wooing time of life!
The sweet wooing time of life!
When the heart with rapture burns,
And the bosom fondly yearns
To solace every sorrow, and to banish every strife;
When the golden age again
Blesses earth, and maids, and men.
Oh, would the power were given,
By the boundless grace of heaven,
For ever to retain the sweet wooing time of life!

SING ON, BONNY BIRD.

Sing on, bonny bird, from thy bloom-covered
    bough ;
  Sing on, bonny bird, with a joy deep as mine ;
'Neath the bee-haunted lime, whence thy song
    ripples now,
  I stood yesternight in a rapture divine.

Sing on, bonny bird, while I tell thee the tale ;
  Sing on, bonny bird, for my heart sings with
    thee ;
Young Edwin, thou know'st, is the pride of the
    vale,
  And Edwin, my bird, is betrothed unto me.

Sing on, bonny bird, for our hearts now are light ;
  Sing on, bonny bird, with thy love-prompted lay ;
For he called me his own, his one pet, and delight ;
  And asked me to love him—and could I say nay ?

Sing on, bonny bird, with thy heart all aflame ;
  Sing on, bonny bird, for the summer is nigh ;
And then the church bells will a bridal proclaim,
  And who in the world be so happy as I ?

Sing on, bonny bird, with thy love in her nest ;
  Sing on, bonny bird, a bright vision I see—
A sweet cottage home, that with true love is blest,
  And the queen in that home, dearest birdie, is
    me !

Sing on, bonny bird, let my joy make thee glad ;
  Sing on, bonny bird, for a footstep I hear ;
With the best of thy singing now welcome my
    lad ;—
  True love to true love should be precious and
    dear.

Sing on, bonny bird, use the time whilst thou may ;
  Sing on, bonny bird, though thy song be of love,
My ears and my heart will be charméd away,
  When my Edwin shall whisper that I am his dove.

Sing on, bonny bird, with thy true love rejoice ;
  Sing on, bonny bird, for my Edwin is near ;
And sweeter than thine are the tones of his voice,
  And sweeter, and dearer, the tale I shall hear.

Sing on, bonny bird, I shall love thee for aye ;
  Sing on, bonny bird, nor our whisperings heed ;
The joy of this moment will ne'er pass away,
  For life will with Edwin be blesséd indeed.

SONG.

———

Oh ! blessed is the power of song !
  Where'er its light may shine,
It fills the heart with peace and love,
  With happiness divine.

Make it thy friend throughout life's course
  Of mingled joy and pain ;
For ever cheering on the heart,
  With some delicious strain.

Come toil or ease ; come joy or care ;
  Whate'er thy lot may be ;
A priceless treasure still is thine,
  If Song remain with thee.

THE ELFIN AND THE PILGRIM.

(From the German of Oelenschläger.)

The Elfin dwells in her cavern hall,
The Pilgrim sits by the waterfall.
The waters plunge, as white as snow,
From the rocky height, deep, deep below.
The Pilgrim leaps in the deep abyss :
" For ever be thou my only bliss.

" My soul from my body I loosen for thee,
Thou shalt merrily dance in the forest with me."
"Sir Pilgrim, plunge in, plunge quickly," she said,
" Thy body as ivory white shall be made.
And deep in my chamber thy rest shall be sound,
While the mountain stream over thee dashes
     around."

Then shudders the Pilgrim, and fain would he rise;
But weak are his limbs, and he powerless lies.
The Elfin stands up with her bright golden hair,
And a beaker of water she offers him there ;
The Pilgrim at once drinks the liquid so clear,
And swiftly with fever he's pallid and sear.

A cold shudder runs through marrow and blood;
A draught he has drunk of Death's own flood;
And now—white he sinks on the roses so red;
The Pilgrim lies on them, the Pilgrim is dead.
Him the whirlpool enfolds as it dashes around;
And there lie his bones on the cold, clammy
    ground.

In sooth now his soul of his body is free,
And night after night to the forest comes she.
In Spring, when more swiftly flows down the hill-
    flood,
His ghost and the Elfin dance light in the wood.
But as through the dark grove beams the morn's
    spectral glow,
His body lies white in the waters below.

WISDOM.

———

" The brightness of the everlasting light,
   Th' unspotted mirror of the power of God,
   And image of His goodness." [1] One who trod
The earth long since, from Truth's serenest height
Saw Wisdom thus ; and, as she blessed his sight,
   These fit similitudes on her bestowed :
   And never since from mortal lips have flowed
More glorious words, more radiantly bright.

Oh, may my heart be filled, like his of old,
   With love unquenchable, and pure, and deep,
   For Wisdom ; may I all her beauty see ;
Preferring her to praise, and fame, and gold ;
   And have the grace her holy laws to keep ;
   Content with little, if she dwell with me.

     [1] Wisdom of Solomon, c. vii.

STORM AND CALM.

The winter wind howls fiercely round the house,
And beats and batters at each rattling pane.
Though baffled oft, it swift returns again,
And wildly shrieks our terror to arouse,
With sounds like demons holding deep carouse,
Or Bacchanals with frenzy-firéd brain.
But vain its fury ; all its powers are vain
To shake the peace we feel, myself and spouse.

For here we sit beside the glowing fire,
And hand in hand recall the bygone days ;
The flowery paths we trod ; the sunny Mays
Which have been ours ; the realized desire,
Whose memory is a theme can never tire.
So calmly love with recollection plays.

TWO LOVE LYRICS.

I.

Why should I sing that I love thee,
　　Since years have approved the truth ?
" On earth is no woman above thee : "
　　Thus whispered the dream of my youth.
And now that the dream is fulfilled,
　　No words can be uttered so sweet ;
With bliss all my being is thrilled,
　　As that love-charm I fondly repeat.

The joy and the pride of my home,
　　The loving-belovéd of all ;
And mem'ry, wherever I roam,
　　Bright visions of thee will recall.
The crown of all bliss is to love thee ;
　　And still I can truly repeat
" On earth is no woman above thee,
　　So perfect, so true, so complete."

II.

Why should I sing that I love thee?
Or utter once more in a rhyme,
"On earth is no woman above thee,
Nor will be till th' ending of time?"
Because it is sweet to thy ear,
Though repeated again and again;
No song of the poet's so dear,
Nor rings with a sweeter refrain.

The lark from the heavens above
Greets his mate sitting low on the ground,
And though ever repeating his love,
Is never monotonous found.
So, dearest, my love-charm is still
Ever new, be it ever so old,
And my heart with all blessing can fill,
No matter how oft it is told.

CONTENT.

I neither toil nor pray for wealth;
No riches covet—only health;
The healthy heart, the healthy hand,
And healthy brain to understand.

With these what need of wealth have I?
The world is mine—earth, sea, and sky;
And every star, and every flower,
To give me pleasure, has the power.

The meanest object I behold
Has teachings rich and manifold;
Can cheer the heart, the spirits raise,
And touch the chords of song and praise.

The sun, the moon, each lucent star,
The birds, the streams, my poets are:
What other pictures need I see,
Than God, the Artist, paints for me?

AFTER HEINE.

———

I sang the love of another,
  And gladly she heard the strain;
'Twas good, she said, like a brother,
  To tell of his passion and pain.

I sang my own love, burning
  Through my heart, and soul, and brain;
She turned away in her scorning,
  Unheeding my passion and pain.

And now we sit clasp'd together,
  Her hand in mine own again,
And around us blossoms the heather,
  And dead are our passion and pain.

THE SWEETEST SONG.

O sweet are the songs of our singing birds—
 The thrush, the linnet, and lark ;
And the king of them all, the nightingale,
 Who sings in the light and the dark !—
But they never, oh never so sweet can be
As the song which my true love singeth to me.

The thrush is so fond of his own rich song,
 That he sings it again and again,
And the heart of his mate as she sits on her nest
 Is thrilled by the rapturous strain :
But it never, oh never so sweet can be
As the song which my true love singeth to me.

The linnet in soft and tremulous song
 Reveals love's pleasure and pain,
And the hearts of all true lovers respond
 To his sweetly musical strain :
But it never, oh never so sweet can be
As the song which my true love singeth to me.

The lark in ecstasy carries his song
 To the glorious gates of the sun,

And all with rapture are filled as they hear
   That river of melody run :
But it never, oh never so sweet can be
As the song which my true love singeth to me.

But sweeter than all, the nightingale,
   In meadow, in wood, and in grove,
Fills heaven and earth, in the blissful night-time,
   With the passionate music of love :
Yet it never, oh never so sweet can be
As the song which my true love singeth to me.

MY PET BIRD.

Little bird, my feathered pet,
'Mid life's stir, and noise, and fret,
Sweet it is to turn to thee,
Ever blithesome, glad, and free;
Singing from the break of day,
Till the sun has passed away;
And thy voice so full and clear,
Ev'n the saddest heart would cheer,
With its glorious minstrelsy,
Nature's gift, dear bird, to thee.
Such a rivulet of song
Flowing on the whole day long,
Trilling forth thy happy heart,
Like the little sprite thou art,
In glad spontaneity,
Rich and full as joy can be,
Till the trembling air around
Sweetly vibrates to the sound,
As, in answer to thy call,
Earth itself grew musical.

Blessèd bird, oft has thy voice
Made the sorrowful rejoice;

In the time of grief and dole,
Which the heart could scarce control,
Thou hast brought a sweet relief,
Chasing from the heart its grief;
Giving solace unto pain;
Cheering still the weary brain.
To the mind oppressed with gloom,
Bowed beneath life's heavy doom,
Oft thy singing will recall
Eden days, before the fall
Which each soul endures in life
Brings the struggle and the strife,
As we pass from childhood's years,
Knowing nought of cares and fears;
Loving life for all it brings,
Singing, as my birdie sings,
From the heart's divine excess,
Of its present happiness.
For all joy about us lies,
In this sinless Paradise,
Childhood's blesséd heritage,
Our earth's only Golden Age.

Oft, dear bird, thy artless strain
Makes me live this life again.
Oft thy song my heart will move

To re-live the days of love,
Days so precious and divine,
Ev'n the memory acts like wine,
Thrilling heart, and blood, and brain,
With a joy that touches pain.
Listening to thy song, I seem
Living in a wakeful dream,
Rambling down a shady lane,
O'er the meadow's flower-strewn plain ;
By the river's rippling side,
With my love, my joy, my pride ;
She and I alone together
In the bright and sunny weather,
Slowly pacing to and fro
With the bliss which lovers know ;
Voices gentle, soft and low,
Sweet as is the streamlet's flow ;
By each look, and touch, and word,
All the heart with rapture stirred.
Oft at gloaming 'neath the trees,
Musical with lightest breeze,
Watching there the setting sun,
Then the stars, as one by one,
They appear to glad the eye,
Glinting in the darkling sky ;
While we wonder what they are,

Worlds on worlds from us so far,
Studding heaven with gems of light,
Making beautiful the night ;
And we deem each world above
Is the home of those who love,
Feeling, as we feel, the bliss,
Whispered word and sealing kiss,
In these precious hours impart
To the rapture-throbbing heart.
Or, once more the Queen of Night
Fills the universe with light,
As before her sovran sway
Every star withdraws its ray,
Leaving her supreme, alone,
Reigning on her heavenly throne ;
Shining there behind the trees,
Softly stirred by lightest breeze,
Laden seem with fruit of gold,
Guarded by no dragon bold.
Such the blissful scenes and hours
Summoned by thy vocal powers ;
Making me, in very sooth,
Feel again the joys of youth.

And a friend thou art to me,
Cheering with thy minstrelsy :

Coming when I speak thy name,
Fearless, happy, docile, tame.
On my finger perching, proud
Of the liberty allowed.
With an arch and pretty grace,
Peering oft into my face ;
Pulling at my beard, and then
Chirping saucily again ;
Spreading all thy feathers out,
Looking angrily about,
With a glance that seemed to say—
" Do not mind, 'tis only play."
Following me from room to room,
Joy expressed in every plume ;
Perching proudly on my head,
As thou wert in triumph led ;
Fluttering both thy wings with glee,
Little piece of vanity,
With thy head, in conscious pride,
Turning quick on either side ;
Seeking admiration, too,
By the tricks which thou canst do ;
Showing in thy conscious ways,
That thou feel'st each word of praise ;
Praise which often I bestow,
Thus my love and thanks to show.

But my debt, whate'er I say,
Fully I can ne'er repay.
More than pet, a friend thou art,
Nestled closely in my heart,
Where I trust thou'lt ever be,
While my life remains to me.

COGITANDA.—I.

I.

Not what I have, but what I am :
  'Tis not the purse, but heart and brain :
A palace may but hide a slave ;
  A lowly hut a king contain.

II.

'Tis not the blind alone who cannot see ;
  But men, with open eyes, in broad daylight,
Walk through this wondrous world, and ever be
  Like children groping in the darkest night.

III.

What though you walk on ice, or burning sand,
  Each step you take will bring you further on :
What matter, though beset on either hand,
  If at the end the victory be won.

IV.

With noble aims make rich thy life,
  An upward pathway keep ;
God did not give the form erect
  To grovel, cringe, and creep.

Yet never pass the lowliest thing,
   Without a sign of love;
For high and low one golden chain
   Links unto God above.

V.

No matter what thy hopes may be,
   How high thy aims, how great thy cause,
Nature will only work for thee
   While thou art true to Nature's laws.

VI.

Stand on thy feet, and learn to walk alone,
   Use thy own hands, and eyes, and heart, and
     brain.
Be monarch of thyself, lord of thy own,
   And not a vassal in a servile train.

VII.

Let others fight for shibboleths and creeds,
   The letter keep which holds the soul in thrall:
The spirit follow thou where'er she leads;
   Accept the truth that dwells within them all.

VIII.

God's laws change not, and blest is he who knows
   How to conform to their unerring sway;

His life is free from vain and empty shows,
    And moves harmoniously from day to day.

IX.

Free-will and Fate !   How vain the strife
    Mankind has waged o'er these !
I still am master of my life,
    Can mould ev'n Fate's decrees,

Am free to think, to act am free,
    To move, or to decline ;
And in the face of Destiny
    Can make my life divine.

The coward calls his weakness Fate,
    And justifies the plea :
The brave man walks erect, elate,
    And *knows* that he is free.

X.

A voice, and not an echo, thou shouldst be,
    However weak and feeble be the tone;
The robin piping on his lowly tree,
    Is worthy as the lark before the throne.

COGITANDA.—II.

I.

There's one thing more lovely than love ;
　More beautiful even than beauty ;
A pleasure all pleasures above—
　The faithful discharging of duty.

II.

All men for freedom loudly cry ;
　What freedom is but few can name ;
For most to others will deny
　What for themselves they proudly claim.

III.

Our needs are few, but many are our wants,
　And measureless desire our being tries :
But God, for wisest purpose, often grants
　What least we wish ; what most we ask denies.

IV.

Though all the world should empty seem,
　And all thy life a failure be,
Despair not ; keep thy hope supreme,
　In thinking of eternity.

V.

O happy heart, which ne'er by doubt was torn,
    Whose childlike faith has never lost its bloom ;
Look not with haste, with anger, or with scorn,
    Upon thy brother struggling in the gloom.

But brother-like stretch forth a helping hand ;
    With loving words his painful efforts cheer ;
Reveal the splendours on life's other strand,
    The glorious goal which is for ever near.

VI.

Work for the many, and the end will be
    That in life's noblest things you help the few ;
Work for the few, and such is Fate's decree,
    That e'en the few are little helped by you.

VII.

Purse-proud, you need not hold your head so high !
    The world is mine as well as thine;
Your gold can only what is gold's worth buy,
    While my possessions are divine.

VIII.

The loveliest thing on earth is children's play,
    So innocent, spontaneous, and bright ;

Oh blessed is the man, whose hairs are grey,
    Who still in childhood's games can find delight !

IX.

By prayer, hope, courage, fortitude are wrought :
    But foolish they who all on prayer rely ;
The great old Puritan this lesson taught—
    Trust in the Lord, but keep your powder dry.

X.

Work with the Lord, or all in vain you pray ;
    Keep clean the heart, or sins will nestle there ;
Foul places cleanse, or fevers still will slay
    Your best-beloved, in spite of ceaseless prayer.

XI.

With many rules bind not the soul,
    Nor e'er the slave of habit be ;
Bow only to the high control
    Of truth and right, with conscience free.

XII.

Hide not thy light !   Of what's been given, give ;
    Though but a little taper, it may shed
Some rays on those who still in darkness live,
    Whose steps, henceforth, may be divinely led.

XIII.

With patience still thy burden bear,
　Though great the load, and rough the way :
He conquers who can wait and dare,
　Nor fears the end, be what it may.

XIV.

Impute not motives ; freely take the good,
　Nor scan too closely why the good is done ;
The hungry never quarrel with their food,
　But eat and are content ; so life is won.

XV.

Count up your stores, and I will count up mine ;
　Let gold and gems be yours to vaunt and prize ;
I've rarer treasures : poesy divine,
　And harvests garnered by the good and wise.

COGITANDA.—III.

How foolish they who call words idle things ;
    The lightest spoken here can never die,
But is borne onward with time-sweeping wings,
    And bears effects through all eternity.

II.

We ponder far too much upon the past ;
    And for the future foolishly we sigh ;
Neglect the present, where our lot is cast,
    Our only certain field-time till we die.

III.

How many generous hearts their goodness hide,
    And in men's eyes but hard and cold appear,
From lack of strength to meet and spurn aside
    The scoffer's gibe, the fool's ignoble sneer.

IV.

Our grief is oft at best a selfish grief ;
    We mourn, but 'tis for our own loss we mourn :
And it is well.   The living find relief
    In tears when for the dead the heart is torn.

*   *   *   *

It cannot help the dead. Serene they lie;
   Nor pain, nor sorrow can affect them more;
But we must bear the bitter agony
   Love knows when reft of its most precious store.

V.

A gloomy day; a stomach out of gear;
   Life's merest trifles with our peace at war;
An empty purse, and quarter-day so near;
   A friend proved false, and pessimists we are.

VI.

A sunny sky; a pulse in healthy play;
   Digestion good, and love our guiding star;
A happy home, with friends and children gay—
   How sweet is life, what optimists we are.

VII.

When we invade, attack, subdue, and slay,
   We write it down " A glorious victory;"
But should the foe resist, dispute our sway,
   And slaughter us, " a massacre" we cry.

VIII.

When we've done wrong, and thence are ill at ease,
   How quick at other's faults we angry grow;

And self-accusing conscience to appease,
    Make haste to be the first the stone to throw.

IX.

Still, by its fruit, Christ said, you know the tree ;
    Who does the Father's will is also Son ;
Not so, say priests, you must believe as we,
    For only by our faith is safety won.

X.

Organic things from low to higher rise,
    A still-ascending scale is Nature's plan ;
Beginning with the simplest atomies,
    And ending in the crowning glory, man.

    *   *   *   *

Yet can we say this is in truth the end ?
    Or at this crown must evolution rest ?
For death itself may be indeed the friend
    To lead to life still higher and more blest.

    *   *   *   *

From high to higher still life will ascend,
    Through worlds which even yet we cannot see ;
For who can deem that consciousness will end,
    Nor gain perfection in eternity ?

XI.

"More light !" the poet said, and passed away ;
  Like his, our cry should always be "more light;"
We need it even on the brightest day,
  Much more to guide us through the dark of night.

XII.

One prayer above all prayers a man should pray,
  Not seeking any vain or temporal thing;
Nor wealth, nor pleasure, lasting but a day,
  But strength to bear whatever life may bring,

COGITANDA.—IV.

I.

Art for Art's sake, and Song for Song's, no more !
  Then Art and Song have but an earthly goal,
Will never reach the bright celestial shore,
  Which still demands the all-sustaining soul.

II.

All things that are exist but for the good ;
  Thence all things beautiful and lovely flow.
This vital truth wise Plato understood,
  And taught the world two thousand years ago.

III.

We conquer time and space, throw wide the door ;
  Our lightning messages outstrip the wind;
But thought is swifter far, is there before,
  Though Science boasts, yet still she halts behind.

IV.

The smallest hair its shadow throws : " [1]
With God is neither great nor small :
The weed that in the desert grows,
  Or dew-drop proves the All-in-All.

  [1] Das kleinste Haar wirf seinen Schatten.—*Goethe.*

V.

The brave heart knows not failure or despair ;
 For striving more than winning brings delight,
Turns loss to gain, and makes him but prepare
 For nobler action, and for higher flight.

VI.

The shadow for the substance ! how, alas,
 In the fierce strife for wealth will men pursue !
The things which most enrich the soul will pass,
 Securing those whose gain they most will rue.

VII.

Who works in joy will be supremely blest,
 And all he does will strengthen heart and brain ;
His labour o'er secure will be his rest,
 And life for him be bright in sun or rain.

VIII.

When any one another 'doxy takes,
 " Pervert " we call him in contempt and scorn ;
But if for ours the old one he forsakes,
 " Convert " he is, a child of grace, new-born.

K

IX.

Nature is always kind in storm or calm;
    Her blows are chastening wounds which strength
      impart;
Her tenderness for every heart is balm,
    And fills with pleasure pulse, and brain, and heart.

X.

Each in his little course all lives may live,
    For he the past can to the present bring,
Make every soul his dearest treasures give—
    Be warrior, statesman, poet, priest, or king.

XI.

" To find the mind's construction in the face
    There is no art."   Yet Nature lends her aid:
And rogue, or knave, or fool, in eyes we trace,
    And so the cherished secret is betrayed.

XII.

My friend is mine: is mine through all the years;
    Whilst I am I, can know nor change nor shock.
Love makes him mine above all hopes or fears,
    As strong as fate, less plastic than the rock.

XIII.

Tis strange that men should ever sink so low
　　To utter ribaldry on sacred things ;
But stranger still, that men have yet to know
　　That persecution never gives them wings.

XIV.

Why care so much for praise or blame,
　　Be troubled by the people's tongue ?
Your acts alone can bring you shame,
　　Or honour that is worth a song.